CORNED FLAKES

A Jokebook about Corny Jokes

Frank Maverick 2

PAGE PUBLISHING, INC.
Conneaut Lake, PA

First originally published by Page Publishing 2020

ISBN 978-1-6624-1122-9 (pbk)
ISBN 978-1-6624-1123-6 (digital)

Printed in the United States of America

UNDER PENALTY OF LAW
THIS TAG NOT TO BE
REMOVED EXCEPT BY THE
CONSUMER

But I WARN you; do NOT EAT
(Or CONSUME)
this NOTICE!
It's made of PAPER…
Just LOOK at it and you will be
CHARGED accordingly…
IT's "PAPER-VIEW" (pay-per-view)! Ha ha! LOL!

This book is dedicated to my parents… I would've
handwritten this manuscript, but you'd have
said "MAN-U-SCRIPT'LED" it
(scribbled it)! Ha ha! LOL!
It is also dedicated to all my fans everywhere;
THANKS for your SUPPORT!

I "ROCK"!!!

Sincerely,
FRANK MAVERICK 2

FOREWORD

and Backward…
FRANK MAVERICK 2

About the AUTHOR
FRANK MAVERICK 2/work history…
This is "HIS STORY."

<u>1965–1968</u> NEWS HERALD…
home delivery carrier
<u>1968–1972</u> CENTER BEVERAGE & DELI…
Stock boy/worked forty hours per
week during high school… 4:00 p.m.–
10:00 p.m., 7 days/week, $1.35 per hour.
<u>1970–1972</u> SHERWIN WILLIAMS…
Stock boy/worked 20 hours/week at
SAME TIME as Center Bev (located
next door) $2.25 per hour.

1972–1981 BEEF CORRAL... (1972–1974 Vine Street) started as dishwasher... (Promoted to assistant manager two months later.) (1974–1981) PUBLIC SQUARE/head manager (open 11:00 a.m.–6:00 p.m. MON–SAT) averaged $3,000 daily in sales... Sold OVER 1,000 FISH SAND every Friday and OVER 1,000 CORNED BEEF on ST. PATTY'S DAY.

1981–1990 SISTERS CHICKEN & BISCUITS... (1981–1983, assistant manager; 1983–1990, head manager); MANAGER of the YEAR, four times; second place, two times; and fourth place, one time, finish in seven years as head manager (thirty-six stores competing).

1990–1991 PIZZA HUT Route 615 in Mentor. *MOST IMPROVED STORE of the YEAR in 1991.

1991–1994 RENT-A-CENTER-ACCOUNT MANAGER OF THE YEAR '92, '93, '94

1995–2016 US POSTAL SERVICE—Clerk (2) Certificates of Appreciation... Retired February 29, 2016.

2016–PRESENT COMEDIAN (I'm
   now into FUNNY BUSINESS).
   *First place on first live appearance on stage
   at CHICAGO IMPROV (October 2018).
   *Second show was at CLEVE IMPROV
   (November 2018), also first place…
   *Appeared again at CLEVE IMPROV
   (January 2019), second place…

I actually TIED for first place, but because I used
an "inappropriate" word onstage, I was BANNED
from any further appearances at the IMPROVs…
I learned a valuable lesson—the manager had
informed me not to use such words. But the
other comics suggested I use it, that it would be
FUNNY! I learned to LISTEN to the BOSS,
"NOT" my peers, and to tell jokes according to
my audience… I learned to tell humor that does
NOT OFFEND anyone—GOOD, CLEAN
FAMILY HUMOR that everyone can enjoy.
Not everyone enjoys "CORNY"
HUMOR… Some people
LAUGH at ME instead of the jokes…

But whether you are LAFF'N with me or at me,
I accomplished my GOAL in LIFE…
to make you
LAUGH!
Ha ha! LOL!

FOOD FOR THOUGHT
I thought I wanted food!

I bought tacos at TACO "BELL," but I couldn't
hear the "BELL," so I took 'em back… At first,
the clerk didn't want to take 'em back 'cause I
had thrown away the receipt, but he remembered
me 'cause I had told him a few jokes! Then
he said, "You ring a 'BELL'! Ha ha! LOL!"

I saw a sign outside KFC that said "$20
FILL UP." So I told them I needed GAS! Ha
ha! LOL! But I don't tell people that I get
"gas" at KFC 'cause it'd be bad publicity!

You don't see WENDY on their commercials
anymore 'cause "THE BACON-ATE-'ER!"

I've got news for you; I put "Sliders" from ARBY'S
on my tray, and they didn't "MOVE" at all!

Most CHINESE RESTAURANTS deliver
food, but I don't order delivery… I don't live
close enough for them to "WOK" (walk)
to my apartment III! Ha ha! LOL!

It must be COLD in Long John Silvers Restaurants.
The employees have to wear
SILVER LONG JOHNS!

Popeye's Chicken should sell
spinach, 'cause "POPEYE"
ate spinach… But maybe that's
why they don't sell it;
he eats it all!

Does Popeye's cook their chicken in "olive oil"?
Or does "OLIVE OIL" cook their chicken?
Their baby was named "SWEET PEA."
Sweet peas are not on the drive-through menu;
they're only available when "URINE" the
inside of the store (restroom)! Ha ha! LOL!
"POPEYE'S CHICKEN" is not
an accurate description for
the restaurant; "POPEYE" wasn't
really "CHICKEN,"
especially after he ate his spinach!

I ordered an "impossible whopper"
at BURGER KING.
I asked them if they "had a 'BEEF' with my order."

That's just a "nugget" of information
I thought I'd tell you.
Ha ha! LOL!

I told the waitress at "CRACKER
BARREL" a few jokes.
She said that I "CRACK-'ER" up and that
I'm a "BARREL" of laughs! Ha ha! LOL!

Employees at PIZZA HUT make
a lotta "DOUGH" ($$$).
I was gonna order pizza at
DOMINO'S, but I don't know
how to play that game!
I ordered pizza and a little "CAESAR'S SALAD"
at LITTLE CAESAR'S!

I went into "SUBWAY" but was told that they didn't
have any TRAINS from CLEVE to NY!
I filed a complaint "OVER A FOOT-LONG"!
Ha ha! LOL!

I was gonna go to CULINARY
ARTS SCHOOL to become
a CHEF. But I heard you needed *350 DEGREES*
(oven temperature) to GRADUATE! Ha ha!

LOL! I "simmered" about it but reached my "boil'n point" when I heard that I'd "meat" a lotta people, but some are spoiled rotten!

I never put "zucchini" in the bottom of my shopping cart. It might get "squashed"!

If you order "spare ribs" at the butcher, why aren't they FREE? (If they're SPARE!)

I put a lot of SALT on my food… When I "FART," it's like "SMELLING SALTS"! Ha ha! LOL!

What do you call a cow lying down?
GROUND BEEF! If his name is
Chuck, he's GROUND CHUCK!
What if a ROACH crawls on him?
ROACH (roast) BEEF!
A cow eating CORN is CORNED BEEF!

Not too many people talk about the cow in the "WIZARD OF OZ." He's the COWardly LION. (Oops, I'm LION [lying]; that's an "UDDER" [other] STORY!)

Some libraries in major cities have BIG STONE
STATUES of "LIONS" outside on the front steps.
Take this book out there and SIT on the STEPS
and "READ BETWEEN the LIONS" (lines)!
Why are they a LION (lying)?
Well, it is called a <u>"LIE-BRARY"</u>!

GONE FISH'N
Fish jokes for the Angler!
See the FISH WORLD
from my angle!

I bought my teacher an aquarium…
'cause I heard fish swim in schools!
Ha ha! LOL!

SOMETH'NS "FISHY"

Why was the bulletin board afraid of the shark?
'Cause he was afraid of "a-TACK"! Ha ha! LOL!

Have you ever seen a man-eating fish? Go to RED
LOBSTER and look at the guy sitting next to you.
That's a MAN-EATING FISH!

I went to SAM & ELLA'S (salmonella) DINER
and ordered fish sticks 'cause the fish sticks to
my ribs. The chef got mad 'cause the fish sticks
to the pan when he cooks it! Ha ha! LOL!

Why was the MORON fisherman glad
when the shark attacked him? 'Cause it
was the first BITE he'd gotten all day!
But MORON (more on) that later… Ha ha! LOL!

A SHARK sang for his supper and carried
a TUNA 'round with him the rest of the
day… The TUNA MELT'd in his mouth as
he ate it with a WRY smile on his face…
Thus, he had a TUNA MELT on RYE!

A man caught fish using a COMPUTER... He used the IN-TER-NET approach! Ha ha! LOL!

The fish SMOKED OYSTERS and STEWED about it (oyster stew) but CLAMMED up about it when he went to the DOC (dock)! Ha ha! LOL!

A SHARK ate a CARP in a TUNNEL and got CARPAL TUNNEL!

HOLY MACKEREL... What's a CATFISH served up on a SILVER PLATTER? A PLATTERPUSS! He ate it as an ON TRAY (entrée)!

A fish swam into a WALL and hit his EYE. It was WALLEYE! He then swam into a PINK PORPOISE and got PINK EYE! I told you that on PORPOISE!

The INCREDIBLE HULK fought a SHARK that ripped his SHIRT off him, making him a BAR-A-CUDA!

A FIN is slang for five dollars in some countries... FISH have FINS, so they don't get SHORTCHANGED at mealtime!

The FISH swallowed a CANDLE so he'd
have a PAIR-A-FINS (candle paraffin)!

RED RIDING HOOD decided to go for a
swim on the way to Grandma's house. A SHARK
approached her, and she said, "My, what BIG EYES
you have!" He replied, "The better to SEE you
with, my dear! I SEE YOU, and when I'm done
with you, you'll be in ICU (intensive care unit)!"
RED said, "My, what BIG TEETH you have!"
"The better to CHEWS my victims!" he replied.

A family of TURTLES played a trick on a
SHARK so it wouldn't eat them. They played
the SHELL GAME so he couldn't figure
out which SHELL they were under!

The LITTLE turtle is a comedian; I thought you
might like a "LITTLE" turtle humor! His favorite
joke is about a SKUNK; he says this poor creature
can't do anything right—he STINKS at everything!

A SQUID was almost attacked by a
SHARK, but he stopped so suddenly and
sped away; it left SQUID MARKS!

What happened when the TEENAGE
WHALE swam too close to SHORE? He
got GROUNDED! Ha ha! LOL!

What did the WHALE say when
he swallowed a FROG?
He couldn't TALK; he had a
FROG in his THROAT!

What happened when a FISH ate a MATTA?
(What's a matta?)
He got a bellyache; that's what's a MATTA!
Ha ha! LOL!

A SHARK chewed a HIPPY into three PEACE'S!

The SHARK bit a FISH'S TAIL off, and the FISH
hadda go to a RE-TAIL store! Ha ha! LOL!

How'd the SHARK make money?
He ate GOLDFISH!

The SHARK swallowed a TENNIS
BALL and was taken to COURT 'cause
of all the RACKET it made!

I don't have to worry about getting
eaten by a SHARK; they think
COMEDIANS "TASTE FUNNY"!
Ha ha! LOL!

I went fish'n on a ranch behind BURGER KING…
I caught a "WHOPPER" and two "small fries"!
I took the WHOPPER FISH to the clerk and
asked if they would make me a few sandwiches
out of it. As the cook WRAPPED 'em, he was
SINGING. Thus, he was a RAPPER! Ha ha! LOL!
Did you know that I don't like RAPPERS?
I ONLY "EAT the FOOD"!
Ha ha! LOL!

I am under a LOT of "PIER PRESSURE" to
think up a NEW JOKE every day. Not to worry;
GOD inspires me daily! I ask God, "CANOE
help me, please!" I've had quite an "OAR-
DEAL" trying to buy a BOAT PADDLE!
FISH and Company STINK after three days!
Ha ha! LOL!

I bought this SAILBOAT 'cause there
was a "BIG SALE" (SAIL) on it! I didn't
"MISS the BOAT." And "SCHOONER or
LATER," you'dve figured that out anyway!
Ha ha! LOL!

IT'S A
DOG-EAT-DOG
WORLD!

But don't
eat these "HOT DOGS"!
tr-<u>EAT</u> them like they are…
man's best friend!

"HOT DOGS!"

My dog got a new job. He's a
roofer. Roof, roof, roof!

First day on the job, he came home and
told me he had a ruff, ruff day!

I got him a "shingles" vaccination 'cause he's up on
the shingles all day! But he still got "sick as a dog"!

He accidentally fell off the ladder and
broke his tail. They say, "Every dog has his
day." But now he has a "week-end!"

My dog uses toiletries. He goes to the toilet on trees!

My dog will never win *Dancing with the Stars*.
That's 'cause he has "two left feet!" Ha ha! LOL!
Actually, those aren't feet; they are paws.
So "pause" for a moment before you continue!

My DOG wears the PANTS in our family.
His pants have DOG TAGS on them,
and my DOG TAGS along when we go for walks,
and He PANTS real LOUD!

I was gonna take my dog to a DOG PARK, but
he doesn't own a CAR to PARK it! Ha ha! LOL!

I bought a WATCHDOG… He watches reruns
of LASSIE. I told you he was a WATCHDOG—
he WATCHES a DOG on TV! Ha ha! LOL!

I got a pet dog… I named him PEAVE…
He's a "PET PEAVE" of mine!

A lady's dog ran away. She was gonna put an ad in
the paper but said, "What's the use? He can't read!"

I got a dog; his name is ROVER. He's soft
and fluffy and brown all OVER. He's as
cute and cuddly as SUGAR BABIES; it's
just too bad that he's got RABIES!

My COLLIE likes to eat MELONS.
But he is SAD when he eats them. He's
a very MELANCHOLY dog!

My dog is a BUSINESSMAN. He does
his BUSINESS in my BACKYARD!
Ha ha! LOL!

I had to buy my dog six shoes. I bought him as
a puppy, and he's grown "TWO FEET" since!
I tried to OUTRUN him, but he "LAPPED" me!
Ha ha! LOL!

My female dog WASTES a lotta BAGS…
Her name is "MISSY" ('cause she misses the bags; I
put 'em on the ground, but she doesn't go in 'em!).
Luckily, I can get FREE "doggy bags" at restaurants!

WHEN CONSIDERING BUYING
or ADOPTING A DOG:

Remember that Golden Retrievers
are the best to own…
They retrieve gold for you, thus
providing income for
you to buy them food, treats,
medical attention if they
"fall off the roof" and other necessities!

But beware of a foolish Golden
Retriever; they retrieve
"fool's gold"! Ha ha! LOL!

Chihuahuas are good to own.
They don't drink water;
they "chew wawwa"!

If you put a Collie in your flower bed, you get "Collie flower"! Ha ha! LOL!

Weiner dogs are good to own in "hot-weather climates." They are "hot" dogs to own…very popular!

I had a Dalmatian… But I spilled "spot remover" on him and haven't seen him since! Ha ha! LOL!

Irish Setters make good baby "setters." Irish have a good sense of humor and will keep baby happy!

"Watchdogs" always know what time it is! Ha ha! LOL!

My Beagle was a "hunting dog." He kept running away, and we were always "hunting for him"!

Beware of letting your Shih Tzu "crap" on a neighbor's lawn or they may "sue" you! Ha ha! LOL!

My dogs "peed" everywhere; there were lots of "Poodles"!

This is a MALE (mail) DOG. Instead of
chasing the "letter carrier" (mail person),
this dog "IS" the LETTER CARRIER!
(See him carrying it in his mouth!)
Ha ha! LOL!

HAPPY HOLIDAYS!

From Frank Maverick 2

***We were so POOR this THANKSGIVING…
We hadda SCRAPE our <u>GREENS</u> off
the <u>WALL</u> at WALL-GREENS!
***We couldn't afford a whole TURKEY, only
a big WING to share. When we PRAYED over
the meal, we had dinner on a *<u>WING and a
PRAYER!</u>* We got the WING from a can of RED
BULL, 'cause with Red Bull, you get WIINGS!
***We couldn't afford HAM, so I *<u>HAMM'ed</u>*
it up tell'n JOKES! And I'*<u>YAM'</u>* very funny!
***Once I got started, I got on a *<u>ROLL</u>*. But one
roll wasn't enough for everybody, so I got everyone
ROLL'N-on-the-GROUND laff'n at my jokes!

It was RAINING on Christmas… Santa
called Mrs. Clause and said, "I can SEE
the 'RAIN, DEAR' [reindeer]!"

HAPPY *<u>EAST</u>*-ER, HAPPY *<u>WEST</u>*-ER; wait'll
you read the *"<u>WEST-ER</u>"* (rest of) my jokes!
Ha ha! LOL!

Did you know that GHOSTS get *"<u>DRUNK</u>"* on
HALLOWEEN?
They're full of *<u>BOO'-ZE!</u>*
They also drink heavily on the *<u>Fourth of JULY</u>*.

They drink a *"FIFTH" on the Fourth:*
"DRINKING" themselves to "DEATH"…
That's how they became a GHOST…
"HAUNTING" them forever!

My NEW YEAR'S *RESOLUTION*
every year is to say
"HI" to everyone I see
so they can see me in *"HI-RESOLUTION"!*
Ha ha! LOL!

KETCHUP

I'll "KETCHUP" with you later…

IODIZED SALT

as I a "SALT" you with jokes.

PEPPER

I'll "PEPPER" you with my brand
of quality comedy…

CRUSHED RED PEPPER

If you don't LAUGH, I'll be "CRUSHED."

YELLOW MUSTARD

I'll "MUSTARD" up more jokes…

SWEET RELISH

I "RELISH" tell'n 'em!

REAL MAYONNAISE

I've been telling REAL original
funny jokes since May '00.

HOT SAUCE

Sorry, I've been HITT'N the "SAUCE."
So I'm a little TIPSY right now…

But after all, I am a "RED HOT" comedian…

I'm so "HOT."

I'm on "FIRE."

MILD

And that's a "MILD" way of saying it!

"LETTUCE" laugh today,
And "TOMATO" (tomorrow)…
I'll bet the "RANCH" on it…
As I "DIP" into my assortment of JOKES
That I "LAYS" awake
At night
Think'n up!

I'll be in a "PICKLE" if you don't LAUGH…

Oh, "CHEESE," I could go

on-ion, on-ion, on…

"OLIVE," these are "CONDIMENTS"
of Frank Maverick 2!

Frank Maverick 2, comedian YouTube
and Facebook, different jokes on each
Facebook, like page, new jokes daily

"CANOE," please buy "BOAT" of my books!
**Don't miss the "BOAT," "SCHOONER"
or later you'll buy them anyway!
FRANK MAVERICK 2's second jokebook…
All about BOATS!**

**Please buy this book: there's a
"BIG SAIL" (sale) on it!
It's at "WHOLESALE" price…
'Cause the "WHOLE SAIL" is on it! Ha ha! LOL!**

**Oceangoing Sailboat or Sailboat in Slip
He better be careful, or he'll "SLIP."
It won't make a "SPLASH." It'll be
a "WATERFALL" (water fall).
Ha ha! LOL!
KETCHUP with you LATER!**

hid ames 2

ABOUT THE AUTHOR

Frank Maverick 2, numerous awards for stand-up comedy. It can appeal to all audiences: children, young adults, adults, and the elderly. I can make more than one joke about almost "any" subject!